To Helle, Olav, Ingeborg, and Marie

Library of Congress Cataloging-in-Publication Data
Names: Tjønn, Brynjulf Jung, 1980- author. | Torseter, Øyvind, illustrator.
Title: The most beautiful story / by Brynjulf Jung Tjønn and Øyvind Torseter.
Other titles: Finaste historia. English Description: First English-language edition. |
Brooklyn, NY : Enchanted Lion Books, 2021. | Originally published in Norwegian:
Oslo : Cappelen Damm AS, 2016 under the title, Den Finaste Historia. |
Audience: Ages 4-10. | Audience: Grades 2-3. | Summary: Late at night, Vera runs
to the pond where mysterious, blue-haired Syl tells a wonderful story to bring
Vera's little brother, Salander, back to life again. Identifiers: LCCN 2020049983 |
ISBN 9781592703500 (hardcover)
Subjects: CYAC: Storytelling--Fiction. | Brothers and sisters--Fiction. |
  Life--Fiction. | Death--Fiction.
Classification: LCC PZ7.1.T577 Mos 2021 | DDC [E]--dc23
LC record available at https://lccn.loc.gov/2020049983

www.enchantedlion.com

First English-language edition published in 2021 by Enchanted Lion Books
248 Creamer Street, Studio 4, Brooklyn, NY 11231
First published in Norway as *Den Finaste Historia*
Original Norwegian edition published by Cappelen Damm AS
English-language translation copyright © 2021 by Kari Dickson
Editors, English-language text: Claudia Bedrick, Emilie Robert Wong
All rights reserved under International and Pan-American Copyright Conventions
A CIP is on record with the Library of Congress
ISBN 978-1-59270-350-0
Printed in Italy by Società Editoriale Grafiche AZ

First Printing

BRYNJULF JUNG TJØNN & ØYVIND TORSETER

The Most Beautiful Story

TRANSLATED FROM NORWEGIAN BY KARI DICKSON

Enchanted Lion Books
NEW YORK

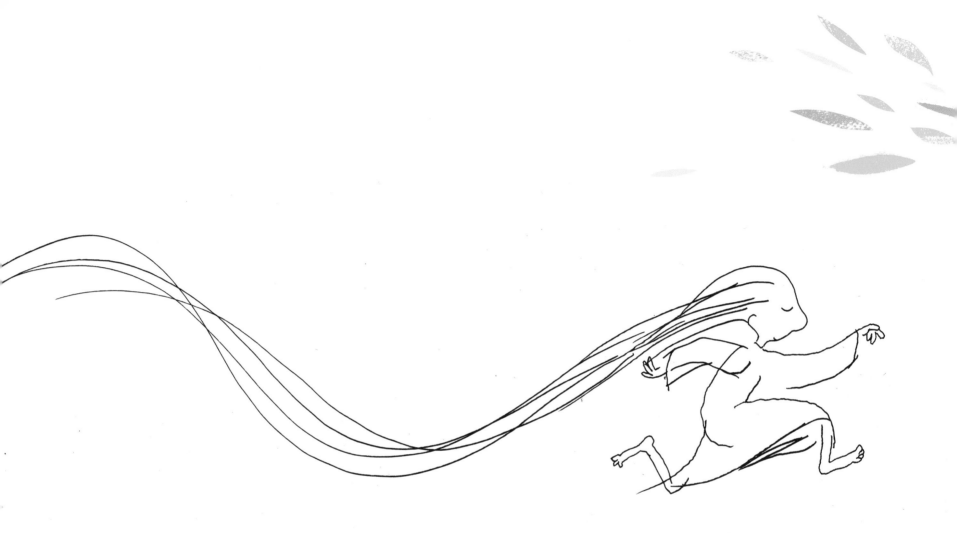

Who is that running
in the middle of the night?

Oh, it's Vera.

Vera and Salander.

On a night when snow has fallen,
on the ground and on the trees.
Look how it glitters in the starlight!

Vera and Salander run.
Like grasshoppers
that need to pee.
Down into the valley.

It's so dark, yet so light.
So cold, yet so warm.

Where are they going?

Are they going to the lake?
At the top of the hill?
Are they really going there?
At this time of night?

Vera and Salander run through the dark.

When all the cars are sleeping.

When the asphalt and dirt are resting.

When the trees are rustling without seeing.

When the flowers are longing for light.

They are going to the lake to meet Syl.
Syl, who tells Vera
the best story ever.
The one where Salander
comes back to life.

Who other than Vera knows
that Syl can make Salander breathe,
and blink his eyes wonderingly,
and move his arms and feet,
his fingers and toes?

When Vera visits Syl,
she can put her ear to Salander's chest
and hear all that his heart has to tell.

That's when his heart is like a murmuring stream.
Like raindrops pounding down.
Like apples hitting the ground.

And Salander smiles,
because Vera wants to listen.

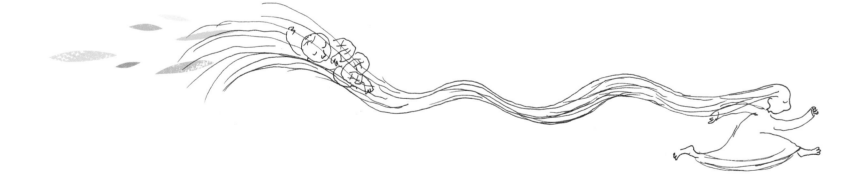

They are on their way!
Leaving behind the house,
where Mom and Dad are asleep.

Vera feels the night's chill
under her bare feet.
Her nightgown is light and billowy.

Vera stops by the edge of the lake,
so close her toes nearly touch the water.

She looks up at the sky.
Then, what normally happens,
happens.

The stars shower down
like warm, whizzing balls of fire.
And there is Syl,
rising out of the lake.

Syl, who is like no one else.
Syl, who is simply herself—
so tender, so resplendent.
With blue hair like birdsong
and such strong hands.

"Welcome, Vera," says Syl.
"Thank you," whispers Vera.

"What can I do for you today?" asks Syl.
"Tell me the most beautiful story," Vera says.
"The one I like best. The one where there is
so much pain, but everything is fine in the end."

Syl tells about the first time Vera came to the lake.

"There was snow in the air."

Syl shapes snowflakes with her hands.

She shakes light from her blue hair.

"There was a cold wind.

There were so many tears.

And such loud wailing.

For there, in the clearing, on the heather, lay a boy."

Syl had seen and heard everything.
Feet racing, flying over the asphalt,
arms trying to grab hold of life.

For there,
his eyes closed,
lay Salander.

Faster, Syl, thinks Vera.
Finish up with the bad part now.

Syl keeps going. "It was night,
and the trees rustled without seeing.
Blue light flashed blueberry in the moonlight.
The asphalt and dirt were pounded awake
from their dreams."

"I went over to him," Syl smiles.
"I pushed the blood into his veins
so it flowed back inside.
Behind his heavy lids,
there were sparks,
and Salander came back to life."

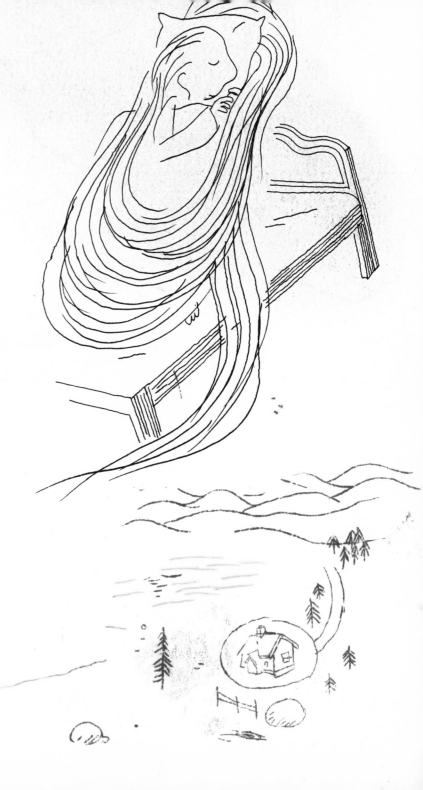

Syl puts her hands
on Salander's heart.
With sparks and flashes of light,
he awakes in Vera's arms.
She puts her ear to his chest
and hears his heart beating.

"Salander," Vera whispers.
"Syl, you saved Salander's life."

"Yes, every time you come to the lake,
 I save him," says Syl.
"I save him a little at a time."

Then Syl sinks down into the lake.
Just as fast as she rose up.

Vera walks home with Salander.
She feels his warm breath on her cheek,
all the way back.

When Vera reaches the house,
she presses her face to Salander's.
His cheeks are still warm.

Mom and Dad are still asleep.
Suddenly, Vera feels a little sad.
Because they don't know
what she knows—
that Salander can breathe,
that his cheeks are as red
as the berries in the forest.